NEVER BRING A ZEBRACORN TO SCHOOL

JACK LEWIS

For information contact:
Starry Dreamer Publishing, LLC 1603 Capitol Ave. Suite 310 A377
Cheyenne, Wyoming 82001
starrydreamerpub@gmail.com

Written by Jack Lewis
Illustrations by Tincho Schmidt

ISBN: 978-1-952328-87-9 (Paperback) 978-1-952328-57-2 (Hardback)
978-1-952328-90-9 (EPUB)

Library of Congress Cataloging-in-Publication Data is available
10 9 8 7 6 5 4 3 2 1
First Edition: August 2021

STARRY DREAMER PUBLISHING

I would like to share with you
This one important rule:
Never, ever, **EVER**, bring
A Zebracorn to school.

Do not bring him to your class
For Thursday's show and tell,
Or your teacher might just have
A rainbow'd fainting spell.

Then all the children in the class
Would shout and laugh, or bawl,
As the excited Zebracorn
Escapes into the hall.

He might smell the carrots
Cooking in the cafeteria,
And ruin everybody's lunch
Causing mass hysteria.

Do not let him in the gym
When they're playing ball,
He'll do his best to join the fun
But he will pop them ALL!

Finally, he'll flee the gym
As angry teachers give him chase.
The principal and janitor
Would also join the race.

Then to the playground he would dash
And try the swirly slide,
But Zebracorns are way too big
To ever fit inside.

Then just when you think he's done
He can still cause quite a fuss,
When the final bell rings
And he jumps into the bus.

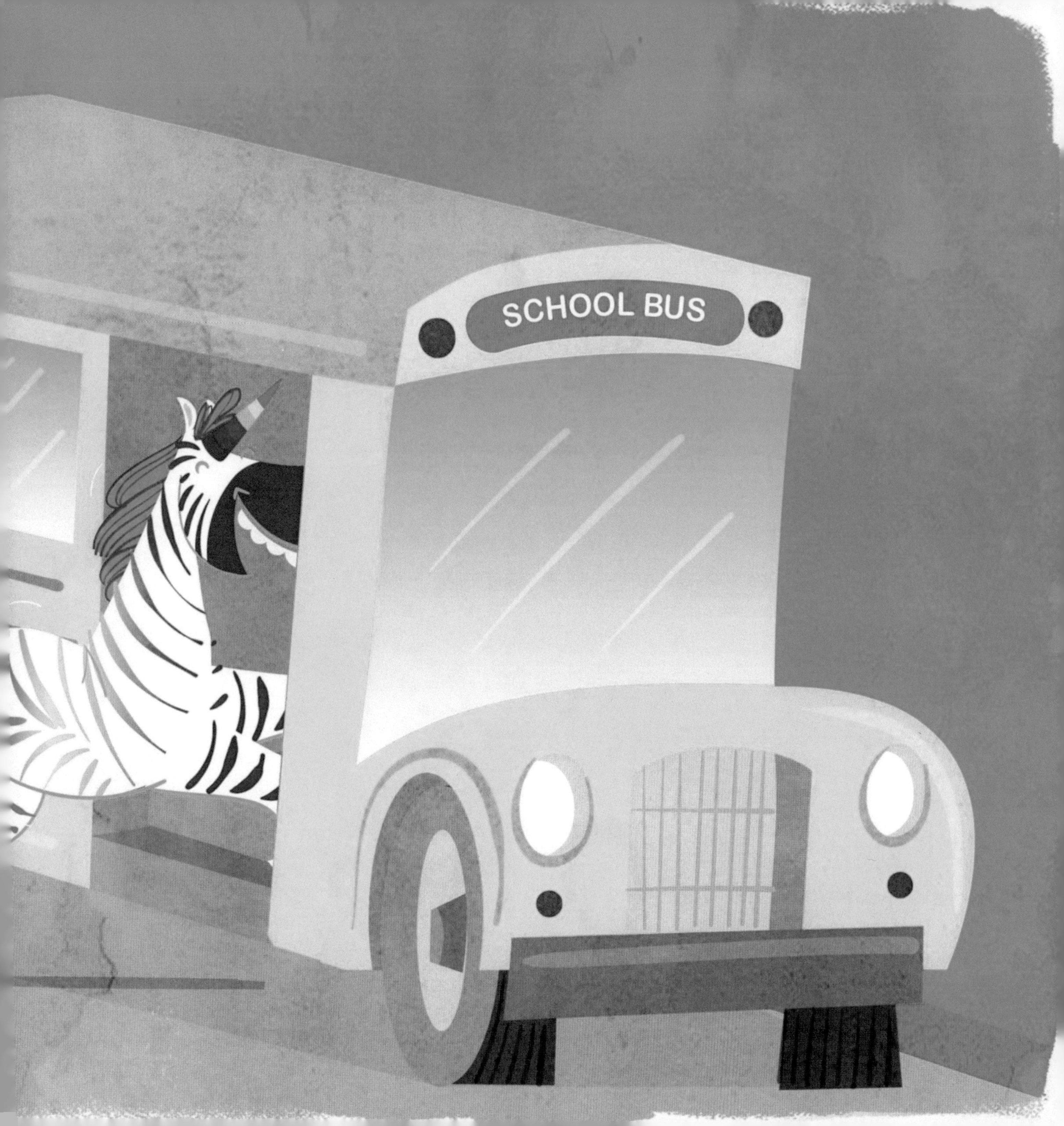
SCHOOL BUS

No matter what you say or do
He won't leave the seat,
Until the driver takes us home
And I bribe him with a treat.

As you can see my Zebracorn
Is quite a naughty pet,
But I still love him anyway
And I'll still tame him yet.

Now I'm sure you understand
The importance of the rule,
To never, ever, EVER bring
A Zebracorn to school.

THE END

Enjoy these other great books by JACK LEWIS:

Joy to the World: The Best Christmas Gift Ever

Christmas is a wonderful time and fun to celebrate, but it means something much more than just colorful decorations, twinkling lights, or wrapped presents. Learn about the gift God gave to the whole world!

Never Bring a Zebracorn to School

Hilarious chaos ensues when a little girl brings her pet Zebracorn to school for show and tell!

Today I Found... Series

Magical children's stories of friendship and the power of imagination!

Today I Found a Unicorn

A young girl's day is turned upside down when she discovers a Unicorn on her lawn!

Today I Found a Mermaid

A regular visit to the beach becomes a magical adventure when you meet a real Mermaid!

Fun with Family Series

A wonderful way to celebrate each special person in our families!

I Love My Mommy

Any day spent with Mommy is a great day! Celebrate the bond between mothers and children with this adorable story.

Made in United States
Orlando, FL
24 April 2024